# If Not Me, Then Who?

## The Tale of the Little Eagle

### Kwame Osei

To order additional copies of this book, contact:
Xlibris LLC
1-888-795-4274
www.Xlibris.com
Orders@Xlibris.com

# Introduction

Have you ever felt out of place, lost in a crowd, doing things you really do not want to do and just desire to be true to who you really are?

**If Not Me, Then Who? – *The Tale of the Little Eagle*** is an inspiring story about an eagle <u>who</u> was raised among pigeons, through circumstances beyond his control.

This story illustrates to young people that they can be more than what their current environment might have them believe. It reveals what can happen when a person decides to be true to his/her identity.

The powerful imagery of the eagle in conjunction with the misconstrued perspective of the pigeon makes this story an unforgettable tale and a must read for youth of all ages.

********

## Which are you? Are you an Eagle or Pigeon?

### EAGLES

Eagles are large, powerful, graceful birds with strong heads and beaks. Eagles are symbols of boldness; they are fast flyers who can soar very high through the sky. Eagles are symbols of power, strength and resilience.

### PIGEONS

Pigeons are birds with firm bodies, short necks, short legs, small heads and slim bills. Although pigeons are high flyers, they spend a lot for their time on the ground feeding off seeds, insects and other waste and garbage from humans. Pigeons are a symbol of peace and contentment.

There once was an eagle family who lived in a mighty tree by a riverbank with soothing waters that continuously flowed to and fro. This family had a father and a soon-to-be mother who had just laid an egg in their cozy little nest that they called home.

It was near summer season; the flowers were blossoming and the bees were buzzing. The father eagle needed to leave to get more wood sticks for the nest, since it was not big enough to support the three of them.

The mother eagle was left alone to tend to her precious egg. She cared for this egg dearly, and guarded it with her life to ensure that it was safe from harm. However, while father eagle was away gathering sticks for the nest, the mother eagle had no choice but to leave the nest and egg all alone to gather up food to prepare for the baby eagle's arrival into the family.

While the mother eagle was away from the nest, a great storm quickly started to form, with gushing, strong winds. The storm was so strong that the wind blew down the entire eagles' nest along with one loud cracking sound of monstrous thunder and rain. The eagle egg fell out of the nest and was carried by the wind until it landed in a pigeon's nest deep in the forest.

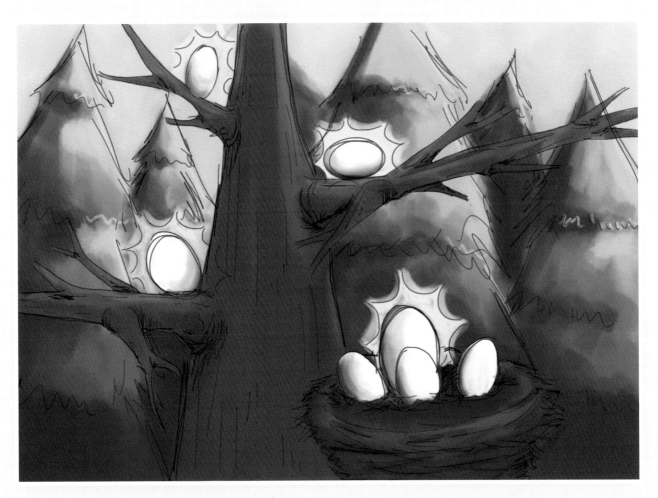

When the storm cleared, the mother of the pigeon's nest took a look at her eggs to see if they were safe. She got confused after she noticed an extra egg was in the nest. She muttered to herself, "I was sure I had three eggs and now there are four; this just does not make any sense! And why is this egg a lot bigger than the others?"

The mother pigeon decided to care and nurture the new egg of the nest as she did her other eggs. As time passed the eggs developed steadily, and they all hatched together. The mother pigeon saw that the baby bird that hatched from the big egg did not look like a pigeon. She then said to herself in confusion, "Hmm he doesn't sound like a pigeon, and he doesn't act like a pigeon either. But he is mine, so I will love him and treat him like one of my own."

As time went on the little eagle grew up with the pigeon family. He lived the life of a pigeon, and did all the things that the pigeons did. He did not do a lot of flying, he ate seeds and garbage left on the ground by humans, he hung out in mall parking lots, he relaxed on high cable lines and watched people pass by. He did this repeatedly with his friends, day in and day out. He never did anything extraordinary, or out of his daily routine. On the outside the eagle clearly looked different from the pigeons, but deep inside, the eagle felt different too. Since the eagle did not know his true self, he just went along with what the other birds were doing.

One day, the little eagle looked up in the sky with amazement and saw a beautiful, powerful eagle with great wings, sturdy claws and a mighty beak, soaring high, free as could be, seemingly on its way to something important.

The little eagle was inspired by the big eagle. He thought to himself, "I wish I could soar freely in the sky and be strong like him, but I could never be like him. I'm just a pigeon, and we don't soar."

Even though the little eagle felt inspired to be like the big powerful eagle, he did not make any changes to his daily routine. He continued to do what pigeons do, day in and day out. However, from the moment he saw the big eagle, he started to feel more and more different from the other pigeons. Something deep down inside the little eagle, was telling him that he didn't quite fit in with his pigeon family anymore and that he was cut out to be something greater.

For the first time, the eagle realized that pigeons didn't do much compared to the big eagle he just saw. Nothing inspired the little eagle about the lives of pigeons.

He realized that he wanted to be independent and he felt the need to do things differently from the way pigeons did, such as hunt for his prey and get first pick instead of eating left overs as he had learned to do from the pigeons.

The little eagle crossed paths with the big powerful eagle once again. Only this time, he had the courage to go up to the eagle and talk to him. He asked him ecstatically, "Mr. Eagle, what does it feel like to be an eagle?" The big eagle was confused. He replied to the little eagle by asking, "What do you mean?"

The little eagle explained, "I wish I could be an eagle like you and soar with great big wings like you do and feel independent and free. But I am just a pigeon. I will never be able to soar high."

The big eagle looked at the little eagle straight in his eyes and said to him with authority, "Do you know you actually ARE an eagle?! You just need to believe you are within yourself and see who you truly are. Only then will you have the courage to soar sky high like me!"

The big eagle continued to motivate the little eagle by saying, "If you continue to hang around with pigeons, then you will never be able to soar like an eagle. If you won't make the change then who will? If you won't challenge yourself to soar, then who will? If not you, then who?"

He went on to say, "If you do not try now? Then when will you try?"

The big eagle guessed correctly and revealed to the little eagle that he had been raised with the pigeon flock his whole life. During this time, the little eagle had been shaped and influenced by his pigeon family and friends and a lot of precious time was wasted doing nothing. The good news was that it was not too late for the little eagle to change.

After speaking with the big eagle, the little eagle took the advice to heart and saw himself for what he could be. He realized that he could soar and rise above any situation. The big eagle taught him to be confident and understand that at the end of the day, the only bird who could stop him from achieving his goals was himself.

The little eagle needed the challenge in order to become who he truly was and so desperately wanted to be. In his attempt to fly higher than he had ever flown before, he flew up and stood on a cable wire and attempted to fly higher, but he was not successful.

He flew to the top of a building and tried to soar from there, but he was not successful; he then made another attempt to fly off a school building, but was once again not successful.

The little eagle tried three times to soar high, and failed. He learned something new through every failure. In all his failed attempts he gained confidence, and was closer to his goal. Finally on his fourth try, standing on the top of a church building, the little eagle thought of the inspiring words of the big eagle and loudly said, "If not me, then who? If not now, then when? If not me, then who!! If not now, then when!!"

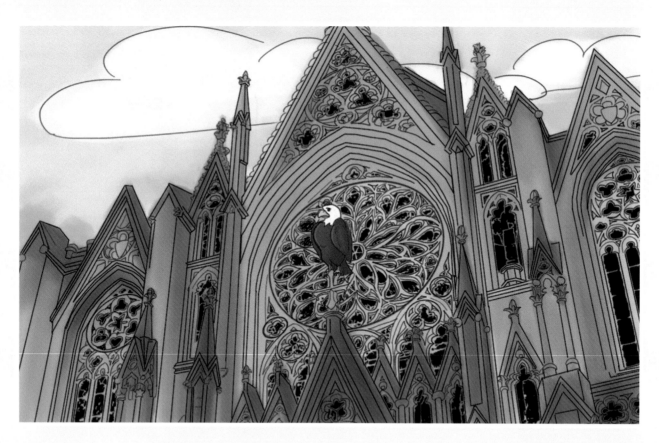

He first spread his wings, leaped off the church roof and with confidence and passion, he began to soar, sky high, and felt that he was on a journey, to something important and great. No one else could have done it but him!

## Message from the Author

During my teen years and as inspiration for writing this book, I considered myself then to be a 'pigeon'. I often let my environment dictate how I acted and how I viewed myself. I thought I was too cool to do anything constructive with my time and myself. I indulged in delinquent behavior and hung around in environments that did not serve me well.

Growing up, I was inspired by the wrong type of images often found in urban society, rather than aligning myself to persons of purpose who were working towards targeted life goals.

When I encounter some young people today, I still come across that same frame of mind in some of them.

I wrote this story, to inspire the young person who hasn't yet identified their worth and to let them know they are truly capable of achieving their hearts desire, if they set their minds to it, and surround themselves around people with the aspirations they admire and want to work towards. Although, this book was meant for the young spirit, its core message will encourage the lives of people of all ages who read it.

CPSIA information can be obtained
at www.ICGtesting.com
Printed in the USA
LVIC06n1736131114
413376LV00002B/2